This book belongs to:

....

For James Mattingly 1926 ~ 2019

A TEMPLAR BOOK

First published in the UK in 2022 by Templar Books,
an imprint of Bonnier Books UK
4th Floor, Victoria House,
Bloomsbury Square, London WC1B 4DA
Owned by Bonnier Books
Sveavägen 56, Stockholm, Sweden
www.bonnierbooks.co.uk

1 3 5 7 9 10 8 6 4 2

ISBN 978-1-80078-119-1 (Hardback)
ISBN 978-1-80078-120-7 (Paperback)

Designed by Genevieve Webster
Edited by Alison Ritchie
Production by Ché Creasey

Printed in China

MIX
Paper from
responsible sources
FSC® C104723

Sam Usher

FOUND

When I woke up
this morning, I was excited –
we were off to the beach!

I said, "Grandad, we can go rock-pooling,

and build the best sandcastle in the world!

And have an ice cream.
And swim in the sea.
And find pirate treasure."

Soon we were ready to go.

I could hear the sea.
Then I could smell the sea.
And then I saw it!

It was a long way down,

but we made it.

We found the perfect spot and set up base.

First we looked for some sea creatures –

and I found one!

Then we started construction . . .

We built for hours.

It was the best sandcastle I'd ever seen!

Grandad said, "I think we deserve
an ice cream, don't you?"

It was the best I'd ever eaten.

"Time to get changed for our swim," Grandad said.

But then we heard something.

"Grandad! It's a baby seal – and it's all tangled up!
We have to help it!"

So we untangled the netting

and borrowed a boat.

We had to take the seal home.

The sky got darker
and the waves got bigger.